James W. Gerard, N.Y. Historical Society

The Old Streets of New York Under the Dutch

A paper read before the New York historical society, June 2 - 1874

James W. Gerard, N.Y. Historical Society

The Old Streets of New York Under the Dutch
A paper read before the New York historical society, June 2 - 1874

ISBN/EAN: 9783337301774

Cover: Foto ©Andreas Hilbeck / pixelio.de

More available books at **www.hansebooks.com**

THE
OLD STREETS

OF

NEW YORK
UNDER THE DUTCH.

A PAPER READ BEFORE THE

NEW YORK HISTORICAL SOCIETY,

June 2, 1874.

BY

JAMES W. GERARD.

NEW YORK:
DOUGLAS TAYLOR, LAW, BOOK AND JOB PRINTER,
Commercial Advertiser Building, cor. Fulton and Nassau Sts

1874

MR. PRESIDENT AND GENTLEMEN

OF THE HISTORICAL SOCIETY:

In venturing to present a sketch of some of the old streets and people of New York, under the Dutch rule, it may be well, first, to glance at antecedent discoveries and settlements in the region by other nations.

Awaking from the sleep of the middle ages, the aroused energy of the European mind, towards the close of the fifteenth century, developed itself in geographical as well as scientific research.

Long intellectual slumber had created a rest which wearied as well as dwarfed.

The invention of printing had distributed knowledge no longer hoarded in cloisters. Improvements in the use of gunpowder tended to subdue caste, and give intellectual as well as civil freedom and vigor.

No longer content with dogmas and traditions, man yearned to break local boundaries and forms—to expand, to learn, to discover.

Marco Paulo's travels had instigated a thirst for adventure; and men's minds were still excited by stories of the wealth and wonders of Cathay and Copango.

The art of navigation had been improved under the leadership of Prince Henry, the Navigator.

New maps were planned. New enterprises stimulated the ambition of the curious or the avaricious. The great problem of the earth was still unsolved. The earth! man's abode and man's study. What was it? What were its limits?

Pythagoras had claimed its rotundity in the mystic days of history. Still, the force of habit and the inertia of ignorance kept concert with error.

The scholastic world still dreamed its old dreams, and wrapped itself in its cloak of Aristotle. Circumnavigation was impossible.

Columbus, however, at the close of the fifteenth century, made the egg stand on its end, and rediscovered the Northmen's lost continent. The shade of Pythagoras triumphed through the Genoese.

Geography vindicated her sister astronomy, and the world *was* round.

The Portuguese, now roused in rivalry, vigorously attacked Eastern realms. Barthalamy Diaz had theretofore reached the southern point of Africa; and Vasco de Gama, in 1497, in searching for the realms of Prester John, carried the Portuguese flag around the African continent, which Pharaoh's vessels had done for the Egyptian flag over 2,000 years before.

The wealth of either Indies now lay open. Unknown El Dorados awaited adventure. Spaniard and Portuguese fiercely claimed the prize of the unknown earth.

Alexander VI. adjudged the great process.

The geographical bulls of 1493 and 1506 made the division for all prospective discovery.

A line from pole to pole was to divide the infidel world between the two most holy navigating powers, who vigorously set to work to utilize the prize.

Magellan, for Spain, in 1519, passed through the straits that bear his name, and circumnavigated the globe.

The Portuguese culled rich productions from Ceylon and the Moluccas, the Persian Gulf, and the coast of Coromandel; while Cortes and Pizarro filled galleons that bore golden fruit to Spain from Mexico and Peru.

Meanwhile the bleak northern coasts lay uncared for. The gold of southern seas and the spicy treasures of the East kept enterprise from them.

England had, in 1497, felt the geographical impulse, and nobly closed the discoveries of the fifteenth century.

The great problem of the day—the northwest passage to India and Cathay through the northern seas (since fruitlessly found by McClure)—turned Henry VII. from affairs of State to win laurels in the new field of geographical research. The Cabots commissioned by him cruised along the North American coast from Labrador to Florida.

Hence England's exclusive claim to the entire country, from these glimpses of the coast by the Cabots.

French fishermen now began to swarm on the Newfoundland Banks, and found there an El Dorado of their own, in savage contrast with Cortez' and Pizarro's sunny conquests.

In 1524, the French appear upon the scene of discovery; and Verrazano carried the French flag from 36 to 50 of north latitude, and named the coast.

Anchoring his ship off The Narrows, in our harbor, as it

is supposed from his description, the Italian, in his shallop, entered our bay.

He says, in his letter to King Francis: " We found a " very pleasant situation among some steep hills, through " which a very large river, deep at its mouth, forced its " way to the sea. We passed up the river about half a " league, when we found it formed a most beautiful lake " three leagues in circuit. All of a sudden a violent, con- " trary wind blew in from the sea, and forced us to return " to our ship, greatly regretting to leave this region, which " seemed so commodious and delightful."

The first of civilized men, Verrazano gazed upon the virgin beauties of our isle, "Manhatta," then slumbering in primeval innocence,—ere long, under the magic hand of civilization, to rise and ripen into stately magnificence, the Queen City of the Hemisphere.

Estevan Gomez, with his Spaniards, succeeded Veraz- zano in the exploration of our bay, and named the North River, San Antonio; after him, also, called on some ancient charts, Rio de Gomez.

We next read of Cartier on the St. Lawrence, and For- bisher and Gilbert in Labrador and Newfoundland; and of Raleigh's colonies at the South, and of Gosnold's failures on the Massachusetts coast, and of King James's sweeping patents to the London and Plymouth companies, embrac- ing territory from Cape Fear to Nova Scotia.

Then of settlements by the Plymouth Company on the Sagadahoc in Maine, whence the adventurous colonists are soon driven homeward by the rigors of the wintry blast.

Then of the Sieur de Monts and his hardy pioneers, under a patent from Henry IV., reaching from Philadelphia to Cape Breton.

While the English and French crowns were thus granting patents of the whole explored region, and settlements were being made North and South, a tract lay between them claimed by both, but settled by neither.

This belt of territory was still uncared for by the European.

There still roamed wild beasts through primeval forests that shadowed a land genial in clime and rich in soil.

There the untamed red man chanted barbaric runes amid dim traditions of his State, unconscious that the force of civilization was at hand, as with the sword of doom, to drive him from his ancient seats.

A new nation now appeared in the arena of discovery.

A people daring, enterprising, persevering—born almost in the sea which they had mastered—descendants of the ancient Norsemen, whose hardihood they inherited—nurtured amid morass and fen—exposed to icy blasts from the North sea and humid exhalations from canal and dyke—taught early and ever to battle with nature or to perish—where the face of sea and land and sky, pale, sad and leaden, gives seriousness to the mind and resolve to the character. With a country less than a quarter the size of this State, this people, in 1579, had made a nation whose character had been formed amid perils and tears and blood.

For over forty years they had battled with the fierce legions of Spain in defence of home and life.

For over forty years they had shown a courage and a perseverance, under trial and defeat, almost unparalleled in human history, and now, the seven "United Provinces of the Netherlands," having established their liberties and consolidated their State, were vieing with the other nations of Europe in schemes of exploration and dominion.

Their naval power was rapidly augmented. They wrested from Spain and Portugal a large portion of their Indian trade. They planted colonies in the islands of the East; they visited realms of sun and snow in furtherance of commerce and discovery, and became the factors and carriers of Europe; they built up a navy that, at one time, checked the Spanish Armada, and at another drove English fleets from the sea, and triumphantly sailed up the Thames.

Hendrick Hudson now appears upon the scene.

In April, 1609, under the direction of the Netherland East India Company, and for the purpose of finding a N. W. passage—that great sea problem of the day—he dared the perils of the Atlantic in the "Half Moon," of 80 tons, with a crew of 20 men. After stopping at various places along the coast, in September, 1609, he brought his little vessel to anchor in what is now the bay of New York.

According to the Indian tradition, on the appearance of the "Half Moon," there was great consternation among the simple aborigines who then inhabited the dense forests where now this city stands. Some thought it an immensely large fish or huge monster of the sea, others that it was a very large house. As it continued to move in a threatening manner towards the land, couriers were sent off to notify the scattered chiefs and their people of the phenomenou, and put them on their guard, and to gather in the warriors. These various Indians arriving in large numbers on the Manhattan shore, and viewing the strange object that was slowly moving toward them, concluded that it was a large canoe or house, in which the great Manitto, or Supreme Being, himself was, and that he was coming to visit them. The chiefs then deliberated in council how the great Manitto should be received. Meat was arranged for sacrifice; the women were directed to prepare the best of victuals; idols or images were anxiously examined and put in order, and a grand dance was prepared, as this was supposed to be not only an agreeable entertainment for the Manitto, but it might contribute to appease him in case he was angry. The conjurors were also set to work to determine what the meaning of the phenomenon was, and what the result would be. To the chiefs and wise men of the nation, women and children were looking up in terror for advice and protection. Between hope and fear, and in confusion, a dance, that great resource of the Indian in difficulty, commenced; and woods and shore rang with the wild and agitated cries of the leaping savages and the loud beat of the tom-tom.

Scouts coming in declare the object to be a house of various colors, and crowded with living creatures. It now appeared certain that it was the great Manitto bringing them some new kind of game. Soon there is hailing from the vessel in a strange tongue. Many now begin to run to the interior woods. The house or large canoe having stopped, a smaller canoe comes ashore with a man altogether red from head to foot, and dressed differently from the others. In the meantime the chiefs and wise men had formed a large circle, and calmly and in resigned silence awaited the awful visitor. The red-clothed man then entered the circle, and we find, by the tradition, that the fear of the savages presently disappeared under the conciliatory deportment of the explorer and his men; and soon, by dint of presents and kind treatment, the best understanding was established, which was continued on the arrival of the vessel in the following season.

Hudson then began the exploration of the " Great River of the Mountains," as it was called, hoping that by it there might be a passage through the continent to the Asiatic seas.

The explorers have left accounts of their expedition up the river, and express delight at its size and the beauty of the scenery, beginning to be clad, as nature then was, in gorgeous hues, shining through the soft haze of the atumnal summer.

Hudson penetrated to the highest point of navigation beyond Albany, and was a month in his exploration. He sent an account of his voyage to his Dutch employers at Amsterdam, stating, among other things, that "it is as beautiful a land as the foot of man can tread upon."

We can imagine the surprise and consternation of the savage tribes that lined the banks as the little "Half Moon," gigantic to them, cautiously crept on its way up the " River of the Mountains "—its motley crew peering over the vessel's sides to gaze upon the wonders and beauties of the strange land, and half mistrusting the savages that gazed back at them from the shore. The daring commander, " the man clothed all in red," we may picture reposing himself, after his long and anxious sea voyage, on the lofty poop, smoking, perhaps, some of the raw tobacco just got from the Indians, and viewing the noble river that was to bear his name. Now he watches the smoke curling up from some wigwam in glade or dell, now admires the frowning battlements of the Palisades, now passing in wonder under the shadow of the "Dunderberg," or the lofty "Crow Nest," or the bold headland since called, as tradition narrates, St. Anthony's Nose, after the nasal organ of Anthony de Hooge, Secretary of the colony of Rensselaerswyck, and marvelling at the depth of the pellucid stream as the little ship wound cautiously through the weird gorges of the highlands, and gazing with the delight of a traveller as he approached the lofty range of the Kaatskills, whose crests, illumined by the sun, came peering through the moving clouds.

Anon, a shot from a Culverin plows through the glassy stream and awakes the silent forests.

The startled deer rush back to inner glades; and wolf and otter, and fox and bear, and basking snake, retreat to den and brake. The eagle shrilly screams, and wheels a further flight, while echoes prolonged resound from shore to shore, and proudest chief, and squaw, and child fall down in dread as they see the lightning flash from the moving house, and hear the sharp thunder that shakes the silence of their ancient abodes.

A quaint extract from an account, written by Robert Juet, one of Hudson's mates, shows the friendly intercourse

2

established by Hudson with the red man as he went up the river, and the ready manner with which they took to the white man's fiery drink, soon the bane of their doomed race :—

"In the afternoon our master's mate went on land with an old savage, a Governor of the Countrie, who carried him to his house, and made him good cheere. * * * * The People of the Countrie came flocking aboard, and brought us grapes and Pompions, which we bought for trifles. * * * Our carpenter went on land and made a foreyard ; and our master and his mate determined to trie some of the chiefe men of the countrie, whether they had any treacherie in them. So they took them down into the cabbin, and gave them so much wine and *Aqua ritæ* that they were all merrie ; and one of them had his wife with him, which sate so modestly as any of our country women would doe in a strange place. In the end one of them was drunke, which had been aboard of our ship all the time that we had been there ; and that was strange to them, for they could not tell how to take it."

The Indians, we read, reciprocated their good treatment by bringing oysters, and fish, and wampum, and other tributes on board.

On Hudson's return down the river, the Indians, becoming more familiar with the moving house, were more inclined to hostility, possibly under some provocation given. Their warlike and venturesome spirit was also aroused to try conclusions with the strange race; and we read further, in Juet's journal, this brief account of the first conflict and bloodshed between the white and red man on these shores, when gunpowder, the new civilizing agent, was employed :

"This afternoon one canoe kept hanging under our sterne, with one man in it, which we could not keep from thence, who got up by our rudder to the cabin window and stole out my pillow and two shirts, and two Bandeleers. Our master's mate shot at him, and stroke him on the brest, and killed him ; whereupon all the rest fled away, some in their canoes, and some leapt out of them into the water. We manned our boat and got our things againe. Then one of them that swamme got hold of our boat, thinking to overthrow it. But our cooke took a sword and cut off one of his hands, and he was drowned."

Another trouble occurred about off the present Nyack, as the vessel was descending the river :

"At break of day," Juet recounts, "we weighed, the wind being at N. West, and got down 7 leagues. Then the flood was come strong, so we anchored. Then came one of the savages that swam away from us at our going up the river, with many others, thinking to betray us. But we perceived their intent, and suffered none of them to enter the ship. Whereupon two canoes full of men, with their bows and arrows, shot at us after our stern ; in recompense whereof we discharged six muskets, and killed two or three of them. Then above a hundred came to a point of land to shoot us. Then I shot a *falcon* at them, and killed two of them ; whereupon the rest fled into the woods. Yet they manned off another canoe with 9 or 10 men, which came to meet us. So that I shot at it also a falcon, and shot it through and killed one of them. Then our men with their muskets killed 3 or 4 more of them. So they went their way."

Hudson's account of the beauty and fertility of the region, and the rich peltry to be obtained there, aroused the attention of his Dutch employers, who immediately started expeditions with a view to settlement and trade.

Voyages were undertaken, at private risk, in 1610 to 1612, to trade with the Indians at and along the river "Mauritius," as it was called after Prince Maurice, and a few houses or huts erected.

A trading house was also established on Castle Island at the west side of the river, a little below the present Albany, and called Fort Nassau.

In 1614 a charter or monopoly of trading was granted by the States-General to an Amsterdam Association, and the territory was recognized for the first time under its new name of "Nieuw Nederland," which comprised the region, as set forth in the charter, between "New France and Virginia, the sea coasts whereof extend from the 40th to the 45th of latitude."

In 1621 an exclusive charter, with almost sovereign powers, was given to the DUTCH WEST INDIA COMPANY. This company immediately began the business of active colonisation and the construction of buildings for the occupation of the colonists, and sent out cattle and farming materials and implements. By the charter the West India Company became the immediate sovereign of New Netherland, subject to the general supervision and control of the States-General, in whom the ultimate sovereignity resided, and to whom allegiance was sworn.

The colony was put under the government of a Director and Council, of whom the Governor or Director was directly commissioned by the States-General. The Council was appointed by the Director with the approbation of the Company.

We read that Peter Minuit, one of the early directors, in 1626, purchased the island of Manhattan, for the Company, from the Indians, for sixty guilders, or about twenty-four dollars.

This amount seems not a very large one for the City of

New York, but, on compounding the interest, it reaches at this time about the sum of one hundred and forty millions of dollars.

The sum of twenty-four dollars, paid in wampum, was doubtless quite satisfactory to the Red man, who had most of the Continent at his disposal; and it is to be remarked that the dealings of our Dutch ancestors with the aborigines was characterized by a rigid regard for their rights, whatever they were, and no title was deemed vested and no right absolutely claimed, until satisfaction to the savage owner was made.

The City of New York at this time, that is to say at fourteen years of age, consisted of less than two score rudely fashioned log-houses extending along the southeast shore, together with one or two buildings of greater importance belonging to the Company, including a simple block house for defence against the red men.

Time will not allow us to go into details of the little colony under its successive directors, May, Verhulst, Minuit, Van Twiller, and Kieft, extending from 1624 to 1647.

The sturdy colonists battled with the wilderness that surrounded them and maintained their little settlement amid danger and privation.

They threw the charms of home and family and peace where for all time had been rude nature and barbaric life. Industry, thrift, and order gave cheerful aspect to the scene, and made success to follow labor.

Little "bouweries" or farms began to spring up even on adjacent shores, and the Metowacks on Sewan-hacky (Long Island), and the Monatons on Staten Island (*Monacknong*),

and the Sanhickans on the Jersey shore, looked on in wonder at the novel implements, the docile cattle, and the
steady industry of the white man, who soon, with fruit and
flower and golden grain, gave bloom and beauty to the
barren land.

Little clearings now were made among the more favorite
situations on the Island along the Hel-gat or East river,
and time-scarred oak and sturdy beach and elm began to
fall before the woodman's axe,that penetrated and resounded
through the hitherto silent mysteries of the woods, and
drove back beast and bird to inner shades.

The size and prosperity of the settlement rapidly increased under thrift and perseverance. Lands were given
to settlers, religious freedom guaranteed, and the tide of
immigration began rapidly to flow.

Of course, while these earlier settlements were being
made, the present city and county presented a highly rural
aspect. A dense forest covered the middle and upper portions of the region, where lived the red man in primitive
barbarism.

Brooks, ponds, swamps, and marshes characterized other
portions of the Island of the "Manhattoes." Lofty hills
were on the site of parts of Beekman and Ferry streets, on
both sides of Maiden Lane, and on the present site of parts
of Nassau, Cedar, and Liberty streets.

A range of sandy hills traversed the city from about
the corner of Charlton and Varick to the junction of
Eighth and Greene streets. North of them ran the
brook or rivulet called by the Indians Minetta, and by
the Dutch " Bestevaer's Killetje," or Grandfather's Brook,

which, coursing through the marshes of Washington Square, emptied into the North River at the foot of Charlton street.

A chain of waters extended from James street at the southeast, to Canal street at the northwest. A ditch and inlet occupied the place of Broad street. Extensive meadow or marsh land, known subsequently as Stuyvesant meadow or swamp, extended from 14th street down to Houston street.

Near the present Tombs in Centre street, was a large pond or lake of fresh water, subsequently called the "*Kalck-hoeck*," with verdant hills and sloping banks. This pond was connected with the East River by a rivulet called the *Versch Water*, or fresh water, running eastward and crossing Chatham between Pearl and Roosevelt streets. An extensive swamp extended north of the present Laight street, subsequently called Lispenard's swamp or meadows, and joined the Kalck-hoeck to the north of that pond.

A marsh also lay between Exchange Place, William and New streets, called the "*Company's Valley*," whose waters were drained by the great ditches in Broad and Beaver streets.

A swamp or marsh also extended over parts of Cherry, James and Catharine streets; and what was subsequently Beekman swamp covered what is still known as "The Swamp," over the region about Ferry and Cliff and Frankfort streets.

The lower part of the island was luxuriant in verdure, rolling and well watered, and invited the colonist to rest there not only by its propinquity to navigation, but by su-

perior fertility and aptitude for culture, and the picturesque
beauty of its situation.

Wolves roamed at large through the wilderness north of
the present park ; and as late as 1685 we read of a gubernatorial proclamation, speaking of the mischief done by
wolves, and giving permission to any inhabitants on the
Island of Manhattan to hunt and destroy them.

On the unsettled portion of the island continued to dwell
and follow the chase, the fierce tribe of the Man-hattas.

Oft the infant colony was startled by the wild hoops of
the red man and the rush of the game, as wolf or deer or
hare, in the ardor of the chase, was driven into the cluster
of cottages that constituted the first settlement on the
island.

Subsequently, difficulties with the red men at times
brought rapine and ruin. The desolating war with the
Indians, initiated through the unwise policy of Gov. Kieft,
lasted nearly five years, with hardly a temporary cessation,
and "Nieuw Amsterdam" became nearly depopulated.
Scarcely one hundred able men besides traders could be
then found. Father Jogues, a Jesuit Father, travelling
there in 1643, speaks of the sufferings of the inhabitants
from the murderous attacks of the red man as "grievous
to see."

During the period above referred to, colonization by the
English had been going on in New England. The colonies
of Plymouth, Massachusetts Bay, Connecticut and New
Haven were established in succession, and occasional com-
munication took place between their officials and the Dutch
Governors on the "Manhattoes," which was conducted with

great courtesy and kindness. In answer to a letter from de Rasières, the Dutch Secretary, which, as a tribute of neighborly kindness, was accompanied by "a rundlett of sugar and two Holland cheeses," William Bradford, the Governor of Plymouth in 1627, expresses himself as follows: "It is our resolution and hearty desire to hold and continue all friendship and good neighborhood with you as far as we may and lies in our power. * * * We cannot likewise omit (out of our love and good affection toward you, and the trust you repose in us) to give you warning of the danger which may befall you, that you may prevent it; for if you light either in the hands of those of Virginia, or the fishing ships which come to Virginia, peradventure they will make prize of you, if they can, if they find you trading within their limits; as they surprised a colony of the French not many years since which was seated within their bounds."

These communications, although always courteous, and generally friendly, even when the home governments were at war, we find always accompanied by a protest or claim by the English that the Dutch were occupying their possessions without legal claim or right, and in opposition to the English title; while the Dutch as persistently retaliated, asserting their claim as founded on Hudson's discovery and a continuous occupation.

I propose now to take a stroll about the City of "Nieuw Amsterdam," sometimes called the town of the "Manhadoes," or "Manhattans," or of the "Manatthanes," the capital of New Netherlands, somewhere about the period between 1658 and 1660, under the administration of his Excellency Petrus Stuyvesant, the last of the Dutch Governors, and a few years before the surrender of the province to the English.

The Governor had returned successful, two or three years before, from his great campaign against Fort Casimer and Fort Christina, and the Swedish settlements on the South or Delaware River; the Indians had been awed into submission, and with the exception of an occasional disturbance by the malcontents among the English settlers on Long Island, or a cloud of apprehension that was continually lowering from New England on the vexed question of territorial rights, the little city was progressing in peace and prosperity.

New Amsterdam at this time contained but 220 houses and a population of about 1,400, among whom it is said there were spoken eighteen different tongues. The greater part of the houses were of wood, covered with reeds or shingles, some of them with wooden chimneys; others, of a more pretentious character, were built of little shiny, yellow, glazed bricks, baked in Holland, variegated with blacker bricks of quaint cross and checkerwork design, and were roofed with red and black tiles.

There were a few residences built of stone, as were the company's store-houses on Winkle street. Nearly all of these houses were placed with their gable ends towards the street; the end of the roofs rising to a peak in successive steps.

Surmounting all was that great comfort of a Dutchman,

revered at home through sad experience of broken dyke
and sea barrier—the weathercock.

These primitive mansions were placed in a straggling
manner—some in thoroughfares, and some at random—
about the quaint little town, which was then mostly comprised in the species of semicircle made by Wall street and
the East and North Rivers.

If we could have penetrated the best room of one of the
better class of the residences of this olden time, we would
have beheld an interior in which the inherited order, thrift,
and cleanliness of the race was pleasingly manifested.

Outside, under projecting eaves, was the " *stoep*," the place
of social interchange and domestic repose.

The bulls-eye in the door, and the small size of the lower
windows, indicated a residence amid peril and apprehension
of the savage foe.

Within, the well-scrubbed snow-white floor is covered
with finest sand drawn in figures and festoons. Above, the
polished oaken rafters are cut in quaint device and motto.

Through the glass doors of the nutwood cupboard shine,
glittering in the sunlight or by the blaze from cheerful
hearth, the generous pewter tankard and two-eared cup, and
portly dram mug, and silver porringer and ladle—relics
brought from the old sea home—and Delft ware tea-pot and
bowl, and a few tiny china cups, wherein the social bohea
is often dealt out to appreciative guests, who knit and gos-
sip between the frequent sips.

At one end, in an alcove, is the great four-posted family
bedstead, the pride of the house, the family heir-loom, en-
deared through associations with the past, on which rest its

two beds of down, and chintz flowered curtains, and intricate patchwork quilt, and silken coverlid—triumphs of domestic thrift and handicraft.

In another place is the great cedar chest, where reposes the valued store of household linen, snow-white and substantial, the good housewife's hereditary dowry, increased by industry, and destined to be apportioned among the blooming maidens of the household, when some Jan or Pieter or Jacobus can muster courage to ask them to leave the paternal roof.

Extending almost along the breadth of the room is the great fire-place of those days, in whose ample embrasure would gather the children and the cats and dogs, and the old negro slave croning out his stories on the long winter eve.

Brass-mounted irons support the blazing pile of solid logs. In front is a brazen fender of intricate design, sent over by Holland friends.

Scenes of Scriptural history are illustrated there by the little blue tiles that line the chimney-piece—Jonah's adventures, and Toby's travels, and Sampson's exploits—while on the lofty mantle, covered with flowered tabby chimney cloth, stands the hour-glass, the old Bible with its brazen ends and clasps, the well-burnished family warming-pan, the best pipe of the master of the house, and his trusty sword and fire-piece, that had often helped to defend his home—that had done good service in the expedition against the savages, with old Jan de la Montagnie, at Heemstede, when Kieft was director—that had fought with Sergeant Rodolf at Pavonia—that had flourished in the great campaign against the castles of Week-quaesgeeks, in the valley of Saw-Mill Creek—and that had participated in the bloodless victory over the Swedes on the South river.

In one corner stands the fire-screen, with its gay designs; in another the best spinning-wheel, curiously inlaid.

Against the wainscoated walls is the round tea-table, with its turned-up leaf, the benches in the windows, and in prim array, each in its accustomed place, are the high-backed chairs of Russia leather, adorned with double rows of brass-headed nails, one or two covered, perhaps, by embroidered back and seat, and trimmed with lace—the work of the dexterous fingers of the good house-wife herself, in earlier days.

On the walls might be seen a little mirror in a narrow ebony frame, and also so framed a few engravings of Holland social life, portraits of some Dutch magnate, or scenes of naval fight—the taking of a galleon from hated Spain, or a broadside conflict between two high-pooped frigates.

Here, too, was the loom from which was made the home-spun cloth that clad the good man and his boys, and made stout petticoats for the girls.

These humble homes were scenes of placid joy and content. No artificial pleasures lured from the domestic scene. The family circle formed a tie of strength, where all were attached, occupied, and happy.

Industry kept off the attacks of weariness and the inroad of vice; and the scenes of beauty that nature exhibited around them—the sports of the chase—the arrival of another ship from Amsterdam, with its varied goods and budget of European news—the rumors of an Indian war or tidings from the New England colonies—kept the inhabitants of the little town far from the stagnation that routine often brings to rural circles.

We will begin our perambulations, if you please, at about the present corner of Broadway at the head of Wall— at the old city gate, called the Land-gate, closed nightly by the city watch, where was the outlet from the city walls or palisades, called the " *Cingel*," running a little north of the line of the present Wall street. These palisades were originally erected for defence against the savages, under Governor Kieft's administration, and subsequently strengthened in 1653, when a war was threatened with New England, and a ditch and rampart constructed inside.

We now turn our face down what is modern Broadway, then called the " *Heere Straat.*" We pass the present site of Trinity Church and Church-yard, then the West India Company's garden, running to the river; on which, on a bank overhanging the stream, were the locust trees, the resort of lad and lass for sentimental walk. Here they viewed together the glories of the bay, illumined with beams of setting sun, or whispered hopes under Dian's light, and listened to music of the wave, breaking over what was then the pebbly shore.

Below, on the west side, were the picturesque mansions and gardens and peach orchard running to the river of the *Schout Fiskael*, Hendrick Van Dyck, whose rosy daughter, Diewertie, might be seen looking over the low-cut door. Then came the fine brick house and orchard of Burgomaster Vandiegrist.

Then we pass the old Dutch Church-yard or burying-ground of the settlement, just above the present Morris street, where many of the rude forefathers of the hamlet still lie—the sturdy pioneers that bore the toil and battle of the earlier time, and carved the way for empire.

Even at this time, in digging foundations in that part of the city, is found some disregarded relic of a former sturdy life.

This venerable abiding place of the earlier dead was sold in building lots, under the advancing spirit of the age, in 1677.

In a goodly house near by dwelt the revered Dominie Megapolensis, of whom we shall have something to say by and by. Also, hereabout, some on the west and some on the east side of the street, were Peter Simkan the tailor, and Jan Joostan the skipper, and Jan Stevenson the schoolmaster, and the tavern of the doughty captain and ex-burgomaster, Martin Cregier, who, reposing after his varied campaigns, was still ready for the tented field.

On the east side of Broadway, going down from Wall, the houses were rather of a meaner order; the proximity of the marsh, or Company's Valley, called "Schaap Waytie," or sheep's walk or pasture, a swampy meadow surrounded by hills, running from Wall street and Exchange Place to Broad and Beaver, not making the east as desirable as was the west side. One of these hills was called "Verletten-berg" Hill, and terminated the little canal that led up Broad street. This name was subsequently converted into "Flattenbarach" Hill.

The movement of the cattle from the highways to this meadow made the then rural path, or *schaap-waytie*, which now is known under the more business-like title of Exchange Place, and was known, under the English *regime*, as Garden street.

This region was drained by the ditches dug on the site of Broad and Beaver, which ditches were the humble origin of these two time-honored streets.

We now pass on our left what was known as the old ditch, the "Bever-graft" or "*straat*," which, east of Broad street, was known as "*De Prince-graft*" or "*straat*." On this street lived many well-to-do citizens, whose national instincts caused them not to dislike a little muddy water.

Passing down Broadway, we come to what was called the "Oblique Road," also the "*Marckrelt-steegie*," or the "*Market-field* path," now still Marketfield street. This road or path led from the Broad street canal to the *marckrelt* or market-place, which was opposite the present Bowling-green, commencing on the east side of Whitehall street, near Stone street, and extending as far up as Beaver.

Here was a busy and bustling place. Besides the market-place on the east, there was the Fort at the foot of Broadway, just south of the present Bowling Green, and the parade in front.

There, also, towards the North river, near Battery Place, was the great town windmill, to which farmers carried their wheat in ox-drawn wains, or on the backs of some of the shaggy horses that were allowed to browse and roam

unchecked around the woods on the upper part of the
island.

Here was a sort of business and social exchange, whence
was distributed the news from New England or Holland, or
the last gossipy rumor of the town—where the Domine's
last sermon was discussed, and where the Burgher's rights
were upheld in argument against the invasions of the
Governor.

At the *Marckrelt* was held, also, the great annual cattle
fair, in October, and beasts driven from *Straatfort* and
New Haven, and Snidhampton and Oosthampton, might be
seen in competition with those raised on the island, or
transported from Heemstede and Esopus and Rensselaerswyck, from *Oost-dorp* (in Westchester) and *Rust-dorp* (now
Jamaica).

Another market was held on Saturdays at the Strand,
near the house of Dr. Hans Kierstede, then on the north
side of Pearl street, at about the foot of Moore street, where
was the weigh-house and the little dock, then the only one
in the town.

At these two markets flocked the country folk, some for
purchase, some for sale; coming in farm carts or on horse
and pillion, or from the Jersey or Long Island shore by the
ferry, or in their own boats. Here bustled the housewife,
battling for a bargain with obstinate vendors from
" Gamoenepa ; " here stood the dusky Indian with his
wampum belt; and here the substantial burgher inter-
changing views with some financial wise trader—mayhap
the price of beaver skins, or a sudden rise in clay pipes.

4

Anchored in the inlet in Broad street, and at the little dock on the Strand, might be seen the shallops and canoes of Indian and country people from Long Island, bringing to the markets veal, pork, butter, cheese, roots and straw, raised on their well-tilled farms; and there was venison, and milk, and tobacco, and peaches, and pork, and smoked "twaelt," or striped bass. There, too, are "Gouanes" oysters, not less than a foot long, as recorded in a journal kept at this period, and cider, and herbs, and melons; and here is Indian maize or Turkey wheat, brought by the *Corchaug*, the *Secatang*, or the *Najack* Indians from their homes on Long Island, from which maize was made the favorite Indian pap or mush, called "*Sapaen*"—also extensively adopted by the Dutch, and still known by that name among us moderns.

Here, too, in rather short but voluminous petticoats, hob-nail shoes, woollen stockings, and kirtle and hood, are the sturdy farmers' *vrouws*, gathered from "*Breuckelen*" and *Vlakte-bos* (Flatbush): and buxom lassies from *Ahasimus*, and *Hoboken-Hacking*, and *New Utrecht*, and *New Amersfoordt* (Flatlands), and Ompoge (Amboy), in close-quilted caps and head-bands, and heavy gold earrings, and copper shoe buckles, vending, and bargaining, and chatting; and there are stout farmers from Sapokanican (now Greenwich), and from the new village of "New Haerlem," and from Vlissingen (now Flushing), and from Boomptie's Hoeck, come to buy cattle or poultry, or seeds for their farms.

There are also drovers from the English settlement on the Sound, who, in their little trading-sloops, had muttered good Puritan prayers as they passed through the trials and perils of the "Hel-gat."

There also, in the season, were "elft" (the modern shad), and the water terrapin, whose good qualities were known, even in those days, by the City officials, as testifies Counsellor Van der Donck, who writes, in 1656, "Some persons prepare delicious dishes from the water terrapin, which is luscious food."

At the little dock, or in the canal in Broad street, we may also see canoes of the Marechkawick Indians living between *Nieuw Amersfoort* and *Breuckelen*, bringing wild turkeys, and quail, and white-headed wild geese, and coots, and whistlers, and blue bills, and pelicans, and eel shovelers.

Jan Evertsen Bout, too, is there from "Gamoenepa;" Farmer Verplanck, too, is there from "de Smit's Valey," now Pearl street; and Hermanus Smeeman, from Bergen; and Jan Pietersen, from Nieuw Haarlem; and George Holmes, the Englishman, from his tobacco plantation at "*Deutle*," now Turtle Bay; and Peter Hartgers, the trader, from the Heeregraft; and Daniel Denton, from Heemstede: and one or two Tappaen Indians from the Hudson river, or a "Sint Sing," with skins of fox and squirrel, or wolf: and perhaps a Raritan or a Hackingsack might be there, with the spoils of the chase, from the Jersey shore; and a Maquaa, with beaver skins, from the valley of the Mohawk. The various little boats and sloops take back, at the close of the day, medicines, Barbadoes rum, called by the Dutch "*Kill-devil*;" also muscovado sugar, "*arrack*" for their punch, and, doubtless, some "Olykoeks" and ginger-bread for the little people; and fresh ribbons and caps for Sunday wear; and stout linsey woolsey stuffs, and perhaps some new pipes to please old Granny in the chimney corner.

The medium of exchange between buyer and seller, at these ancient markets, was of a various character. Sometimes it was beaver, or other skins; sometimes grain; sometimes Dutch guilders, or stuyvers; but the favorite currency, preferred by both Dutch colonist and Indian, as well as by the English settlers—in fact, the great common basis of trading—was wampum, *Sewan*, or *Sewant*.

The best was made by the Indians on Long Island, or Sewan-hackey. That was rated as the truly genuine currency, and found its way over all the marts of trade then established in North America.

A fathom of wampum, so called, was as much as a man could reach between his outstretched arms, and was equal to about four guilders. Strictly speaking, *Sewant* was the generic name for the money. Wampum was the white, and Suckauhock the black beads, which were double the value of the white. The white was made from the stem or stock of the periwinkle, now seldom found; the black, or purple, from the inside shell of the hard clam. It was made into beads strung on the sinews of animals, and polished. Three beads of black, or six of white, as a general thing, equalled a Dutch stuyver, or English penny. This was at about *par*, although there were as many fluctuations and commercial panics affecting this currency as we in these days experience with gold coin.

As an illustration of the varied money for the payment

of labor at the time, we read of a contract made, in 1655, between Egbert Van Borsum, the ferry man on the Long Island side, under which the carpenters were to be paid 550 guilders (about 220 dollars): one-third in beaver skins, one-third in good merchantable wampum, and one-third in good silver coin, and small beer to be drunk during work.

We now come to the *Fort*, pride and glory of New Amsterdam, emblem of home authority, local manifestation of that great sovereign power, their High Mightinesses the States-General—around whose walls the earliest memories of the settlers clustered—on whose bastion floated the flag that recalled the brave Fatherland—before whose walls, on the parade, were drilled the little armies of two or three hundred men that went out to battle—under whose protecting power the young hamlet had nestled, and spread, and grown —that still, even with its few and ancient cannon, and crumbling earth works, and broken bastions, exposed from the river and commanded by heights within, bade stern defiance to both civilized and savage foe.

The first Fort was a mere block-house.

The second Fort was commenced in 1633, and constructed of earth works. It was bounded by the present Bridge, Whitehall and State streets, and the Bowling Green. It had four points or bastions, with no moat outside, but was enclosed with a double row of palisades.

Originally called Fort Amsterdam, under the Dutch; subsequently Fort James, under the Duke of York; changed by Gov. Colve, on the Dutch restoration, to Fort Wilhelm Hendrick; changed by Gov. Andros, to Fort James; by Leisler, to Fort William; by Sloughter, to Fort William

Henry; and afterwards called Fort George—its nomenclature exhibited the varying fortunes and history of New Amsterdam.

Several brick and stone dwellings were located within its walls; among them the governor's brick house, and the church built of stone; a windmill was at one of the bastions, and a high flag-staff, on which the orange, yellow and blue colors of the "Privileged West India Co." were hoisted when any vessel was seen in the bay.

During the Indian war, brought about by the unwise and aggressive policy of Governor Kieft, in 1644, the inhabitants fled to the shelter of the Fort, and established their huts as near as possible to the protecting ramparts. These buildings subsequently remained; and grants of land were made to the holders. Thus was formed a portion of the present Pearl street next to Whitehall street, and also a portion of the latter street.

Those were perilous times in the "Manhadoes."

All the farms and exposed habitations about the Island were destroyed, and their panic-stricken inhabitants were driven into the Fort, where the garrison was not over fifty or sixty men.

The plantations about Westchester and Staten Island, and the blooming "bouwerijs" on the East river, and on the line of the present Chatham street, and at Hoboken, Hacking, Pavonia, Navisink, and Tappaen, were laid waste, and almost every settlement on the west side of the Highlands was destroyed and the inhabitants slaughtered.

The great dramatic event connected with the history of

the Fort was its capitulation to the English in 1664, in a time of peace between England and the Netherlands.

Charles II., as is well known, had given a patent of a large territory to his brother, the Duke of York and Albany, comprehending Long Island and all the lands and rivers from the West side of the Connecticut river to the East side of Delaware Bay.

In September of 1664, accordingly, while the colony was under the direction of Gov. Stuyvesant, Col. Nicolls, the Deputy-Governor appointed to reduce and govern the province for the Duke, with scarcely note of warning, appeared in the bay with a fleet of four ships of nearly 100 guns, and a body of 500 regular soldiers, besides seamen. New Englanders also swelled the invading force, and the services of Long Island settlers and savages were also engaged.

The Dutch colony was quite unprepared to contend with such a force, the Fort being in a dilapidated condition, manned by only 250 soldiers, and commanded by hills within pistol shot.

The little garrison accordingly capitulated, with the honors of war, on the 8th of September. The Governor protested against the act, wishing to fight to the last, and exclaiming to the citizens requesting him to surrender, " I had much rather be carried out dead ! "

The conclusion of Gov. Stuyvesant's reply to the summons of the English to surrender the town, against which they threatened the miseries of war, is worth recalling :

" As touching," he writes. " the threats in your conclusion we have nothing to answer, only that we fear nothing but what God (who is as just as merciful) shall lay upon us; all things being in His gracious disposal; and we may as well be preserved by Him with small forces, as by a great army, which makes us to wish you all happiness and prosperity, and recommend *you* to his protection.

"My lords,

"Your thrice humble and affectionate servant and friend,

"P. STUYVESANT."

A dramatic picture suggests itself, representing a part of the English fleet in the bay between the Fort and Nutten (now Governor's) Island, with its guns trained against the old fortification, whose flag was still flying in the Summer breeze; the other ships landing their troops just below Breuckelen, there combining their forces with the English militia from New England, and crossing the river in boat and barge.

The stout old Governor, standing on one of the outer bastions of the Fort, an artilleryman, with lighted match, at his side, waiting the approach of the invaders. A throng of the notables of the city, Burgomasters, and Schepens, and Burghers, all begging him to surrender, and exhibiting the hopeless condition of New Amsterdam, "encompassed and hemmed in by enemies," where defense was impossible, and the two Domines Megapolensis, father and son, imploring him not to commence hostilities which must end in destruction, and finally leading him between them, protesting and sorrowful, from the ramparts.

The Dutch soldiers marched out of the old Fort, according to the terms of capitulation, with their arms fixed, drums beating, and colors flying, and matches lighted, down Beaver lane to the Waterside, and embarked for Holland.

The English flag was hoisted over the Fort, which then became *Fort James,* and *" Nieuw Amsterdam " " New York."*

After its surrender to the English, the little town settled down, with Dutch stolidity, under its English rulers, whose government was kindly. For eight years it pursued an even course under a Mayor and Aldermen, instead of a *Schout, Borgemeesteren,* and *Schepenen,* until, on the war breaking out between the English and the Dutch in 1672, it was retaken by the latter.

New York thereupon was re-christened by the Dutch Governor Colve "New Orange." The name of New Netherland was restored, and the old fort was re-christened Fort *" Wilhelm Hendrick,"* in honor of the Prince of Orange.

On the subsequent peace, however, between England and Holland, in 1674, the region of New Netherland was finally ceded to the English.

Gov. Andros took possession for the Duke and re-christened "New Amsterdam" as "New York," and the fort again became *" Fort James."*

The fort was also the scene of stirring events during the times of anarchy when Leisler was dictator.

Here, with his own hand, the self-constituted Governor had fired one of the fort guns at the King's troops, as they stood on parade, and in a sort of desperate infatuation began to batter the town.

The old fort, during English colonial times, was the scene of gubernatorial state and show, and here too were fired salutes for His Majesty's birth-day, and for victory over Frenchman and Spaniard.

5

The fort was also the scene of stirring events during our revolutionary period, and changed its flag under the fortunes of the war.

At length, when peace had been established in the land, the services of this venerable servant of Bellona were considered no longer necessary by the "Mayor, Aldermen, and Commonalty," whose utilitarian spirit, in 1788, caused its final destruction and removal. And now no remnant remains of this ancient structure, that rose with the settlement of our island, and saw and shared its changing fortunes.

The Church.

Situated in the fort was the Church, where the purest Calvanism, as determined by the Synod of Dort, was disseminated successively by Domine Michaelius, Domine Bogardus, Domine Backerus, and Domines Megapolensis and Drisius.

The earliest church services of the colony had been held in a spacious room or loft over a horse mill; and religious services were at first conducted by a "*Krank-besoeker*" or consoler of the sick. This room was replaced by a plain barn-like wooden structure in 1633, situated on the north side of the present Pearl street, near Whitehall.

Under Governor Kieft the increasing population of the settlement required better accommodations, and the colonists came to the determination that their New England brethren, who had erected fine meeting-houses in their various settlements, ought not to excel them in this matter.

In 1642, a church edifice was accordingly begun, and

placed within the fort for greater security against the attacks of Indians.

The subscriptions for the new church were accomplished during a merry-making at the marriage of a daughter of Domine Bogardus, and the Governor thought wisely that the hilarity incidental to such an occasion would stimulate the generosity of the wedding guests. A chronicle of the time tells us that, after the fourth or fifth round of drinking, his Excellency, Governor Kieft, started the subscription with a large sum of guilders, and the rest followed his example and "subscribed richly." "Some of them," says De Vries, a then sojourner at the settlement, "well repented it, but nothing availed to excuse."

This Church had twin roofs side by side, and upon the gable end, toward the water, there was a small wooden tower with a bell, which called the good people to their devotions, and was also rung on occasions of warning or rejoicing. There was no clock, but a sun-dial on three sides, and the tower was surmounted by the usual weather-cock.

Domine Everardus Bogardus came over in 1633, with the new Governor Van Twiller. The Domine was a prominent man in those days, next only in importance to the Governor, with whom he was often at loggerheads. Soon after his arrival he was smitten by the attractions of the widow of Roeloff Jansen, then the possessor of the fine farm on the Hudson, and now favorably known to us as Anneke Jans. The Domine led to the hymenial altar that historical personage, of whom we shall have something more to say by-and-by. The Domine was often in contention with the governors of the period, and is recorded, when excited under a difference of opinion with Governor Van Twiller, to have addressed that functionary as a "Child of the Devil."

Bogardus was continually at swords-point, also, with Director Kieft. Kieft charged the Domine with continual intoxication, and a love of strife and slander, and with what must have cut him to the quick, of preaching *stupid* sermons; and sent missives to him of threat and denunciation, and divers orders to show cause why he should not be removed, which orders the Domine treated with open contempt.

The Domine, on the other hand, fulminated against the Governor from the pulpit and elsewhere, and denounced him as a consummate villain; and declared that his (the Domine's) goats were a superior animal to the Director; and boasted, on one occasion, that he would give the Director from the pulpit, on the next Sunday, such a shake as would make them both shudder! Kieft, in retaliation, and to drown the Domine's *anathemas*, would also, at times, have the drum beaten and the cannon discharged from the fort outside the church during service. Those were, indeed, trying times!

The Domine, also, was quite a litigant, and the gossips of the day must have been rarely exercised over their tea-cups with the details and progress of an action brought by him against Anthony Jansen Van Salee, as husband and guardian of his wife, Grietie, for slandering the Domine's wife. It seems Mrs. Anneke Bogardus had, on one occasion, unpleasantly talked about Madame Van Salee; whereupon Madame Van Salee had said that Madame Bogardus, in passing through a muddy part of the town, had displayed her ankles more than was necessary. Under the judgment of the Court, Madame Van Salee had to make declaration in public, at the sounding of the bell, that she knew the minister to be an honest and a pious man, and that she had lied falsely. She was further condemned to pay costs, and three gulden for the poor. This treatment might not be amiss for petty gossips even at the present day.

The Domine, also, was defendant in a slander suit brought against him by Deacon Oloff Stevenson Van Cortlandt, which was of long duration; and the attention of the little town was divided between these stirring events and divers troubles with the New Haven and Hartford colonies in the east, occurring about the same time. Domine Bogardus was finally drowned, together with his old opponent, ex-Director Kieft, they having together sailed in the ship "Princess" for Holland, which was wrecked off the English coast in 1647.

Domine Backerus succeeded Domine Bogardus when Stuyvesant became Governor, in 1647, but left in a year or two, being succeeded by the learned Johannes Megapolensis, with whom was subsequently associated his son Samuel, and Domine Drysius.

We may present to ourselves, for a moment, a picture of a congregation of our New Amsterdam predecessors, gathered together for a morning service in the church in the old fort; Jan Gillesen, the *klink*, or bell-ringer, is lustily pulling at the sonorous little Spanish bell, captured by the Dutch fleet from Porto Rico, whose sounds roll

gently o'er hill and meadow, and reach the settlements on
the Long Island shore. The morning sun is shining
brightly over the bay, which glistens through the trees that
are scattered over the verdant field that rolls between the
bay and the fort, while the cottages, with their high-peaked
roofs, and the windmill by the fort, and a few sheep grazing
in the distance, give a varied aspect to the peaceful scene.
All labor has ceased, the song even of birds seems hushed;
and the calm repose of the Sabbath seems to pervade the
very air, and gives to Nature an additional serenity and
repose. The neatly-clad people, in family groups, slowly
and sedately wend their way through road and rural lane
to the house of worship—some on foot, others on horse-
back, or in vehicles, some landing in boats from distant
settlements or neighboring farms on either river.

Nicassius de Sille, the city "*Schout*," accompanied by
Hendrick Van Bommel, the town crier, is going his rounds
to see that all is quiet and conformed to the sacredness of
the day; to keep the lazy Indians and negroes from fight-
ing or gaming, and the tapsters from selling liquor. In
front, and on the side of the fort, is a concourse of waggons
and horses; some animals let loose to graze on the hill-side
that ran towards the water; others drinking from the
trough supplied by the well before the fort; others cared
for by the negro slave boys, who, proud of their charge,
walk them to and fro, and occasionally take a sly ride from
a complaisant animal.

Now, preceded by old Claes Van Elsland, the Marshal
of the Council (who also fulfilled the functions of sexton
and dog-whipper), and marching between the bowing

people up the aisle, we behold him whose presence repre-
sents the " High and Mighty Lords, the States-General of
the United Netherlands, His Highness of Orange, and the
Noble Lords the Managers of the privileged West India
Company ".—no less a personage, in fact, walking with a
cane, sturdy and erect, in spite of his wooden leg, than his
Excellency *De Heer Directeur Generaal Petrus Stuyvesant*,
Governor of Nieuw Nederland, accompanied by his wife,
the lady Judith, walking stately and prim, as becomes her
position as wife of the great Director ; and by her side old
Dr. Johannes de la Montagnie, ex-Councillor, and now
Vice-Director at Fort Orange (Albany), who has come down
on a visit to talk about state affairs.

Following the Governor is the provincial secretary, Cornelius Van Ruyven, and his wife, Hildegonde, a daughter of
Domine Megapolensis ; and here are the " most worshipful, most prudent, and very discreet," their mightinesses
the Burgomasters and Schepens of New Amsterdam, an-
swering to what are now the mayor, aldermen and common
councilmen. Preceding them to their official pew, with
their velvet cushions brought from the Stad Huys, or City
Hall, is old Matthew de Vos, the Town Marshal.

Walking in portly dignity are the Burgomasters, Oloff
Stevensen Van Cortlandt and Paulus Leedersen Vandiegrist ; and the most worshipful Schepens, Cornelius Steenwyck, Johannes de Peyster, Peter Wolfersen Van Couwenhoven, Isaac de Foreest and Jacob Strycker.

Following them we observe Allard Anthony and Isaac
Bedlow, the prosperous traders ; and Joannes de Witt, the
miller and flour merchant ; and Dr. Hans Kierstede, with

his wife Sara, who was a daughter of Mrs. Anneke Jans Bogardus. And here is Madame Cornelia de Peyster, wife of the Schepen, with her golden-clasped psalm-book hanging from her arm by its golden chain; and the wealthy fur trader, Peter Rudolphus de Vries, and Margaretta Hardenbrook, his bride, who, four years later, married the lively young carpenter, Frederick Phillipse, he, who a few years later became also Lord of Phillipse Manor, on the Hudson, by the Pocantico creek or Mill river, just above Tarrytown. And there was the great English merchant, John Dervall, and his handsome wife, Katherina, the daughter of Burgomaster Oloff Stevensen Van Cortlandt, which lady, in after time, also became a wife of and brought a large fortune to the same lucky Mr. Frederick Phillipse, who then sat humbly in the back benches, little dreaming of the good fortune that was awaiting him by his marriage with the neighboring two rich widows. And here is the substantial merchant, Jerominus Ebbing, and the widow de Huller, to whom he was betrothed, daughter of old Johannes de Laet, one of the original proprietors of Rensselaerswyck; and Madame Margaretta de Riemer, formerly Gravenraedt, just married to Schepen Cornelius Steenwyck; and Mrs. Catherine de Boogh Beekman, daughter of Captain de Boogh, then running the smartest craft on the river, which Mrs. Catherine was married to Wilhelmus Beekman, Director on South river. And here is the widow of the late Secretary, Cornelius Van Tienhoven, whose hat and cane had been found in the North river, which was the last seen of the most unpopular man in Nieuw Amsterdam.

Now enters Mrs. Elizabeth Backer, formerly Van Es, the great fur trader on the Heere-graeft, followed by her little slave boy, Toby, carrying her New Testament with silver clasps.

And here, also, is the young baronet, Sir Henry Moody, son of Lady Deborah Moody from " *Gravesende*," she who left the Massachusetts colony because of her views on infant baptism, and who had twice defended her house against savages in the troublous times.

And come also to hear the Domine are some of the Van Curlers and Gerritsens and Wolfertsens and Stryckers, from New Amersfoordt (Flatlands); and the Suedekors and Elbertsens and Van Hattems, from " *Vlackebosh* " or *Midwout* (Flatbush); and old Lubbertsen Vanderbeck from *Breuckelen*; and Rapeljes and Duryees and Cershous, from the *Waalboght*.

And then follow the rest of the good citizens of the place, both those of the great and the small citizenship, the "Groote Burgerrecht" and the " Kleine Burgerrecht"—Dirck Van Schelluyne the notary, Vanderspiegle the baker, whose two little girls subsequently married, one a DeForeest, and the other Rip Van Dam, the Colonial Lieutenant Governor; and burly Burger Jorisen, the patriotic blacksmith from Hanover Square, the last man, five years later, to advocate resistance to the English, and who abandoned the city in disgust after the surrender.

And then Pieter Cornelius Vanderveer and Mrs Elsje, his wife, the daughter of the great merchant, Govert Lockermans, which Mrs. Elsje subsequently married the unfor-

6

tunate Jacob Leisler. Behind Mrs. Vanderveer were her lively sisters, Marritje and Jannetje, and near by, casting sheep's-eyes at the former, was Master Balthazar Bayard, whom she subsequently married.

After the Domine's exhortation was finished, and a prayer from Domine Drysius, and a psalm had been sung, led by Harmanus Van Hoboken, the schoolmaster and "*zieken-trooster*," or choir-leader, whose voice the widow Marritje Pieters particularly admired, the members of the congregation wended their way over street and path and meadow to their respective homes.

The ladies doffed their Sunday finery and set to work in hearty preparation of the noontide meal.

The last we hear of the old Church is the finding of the stone which had been placed, when it was building, over the door in front. The New York *Magazine*, in 1790, records the finding of this venerable relic in these words :

"June 23. On Monday last, in digging away the foundation of the fort, in this city, a square stone was found among the ruins of a chapel (which formerly stood in the fort), with the following Dutch inscription on it : ' Ao. Do. M.D.CXLII. W. Kieft, Dr. Gr. *Heeft de Gemeenten dese Tempel doen Bouwen.*' In English: ' A. D. 1642. Wm. Kieft, Director General, hath the Commonalty caused to build this temple.'"

This stone was removed, it is reported, to the Reformed Dutch Church in Garden street, now Exchange Place, where it was destroyed in the great fire of 1835.

Quitting the Fort and the *Marckvelt*, we proceed down

the rest of the modern Whitehall street, a part of which was included in the *Marckvelt*.

A part of Whitehall, north of Stone, was also subsequently called "*Beurs straat*," or *Purse* street.

On this street stood the Governor's house, built of stone by Stuyvesant, and called, under the English, the *Whitehall*, which gave the modern name to the street. The grounds extended to the river, where was a dock, to which was moored the Gubernatorial State barge.

Crossing Whitehall is Stone street. This street, between Broad and Whitehall, was originally "*Brouwer straat;*" between Broad and Hanover square, and up Pearl to Wall, it was called "*Hoogh straat*," High street, also "the road to the ferry," it being the nearest direct route from the Fort to the Long Island ferry. The roadway thus made to the ferry was the origin of this street.

The ferry road was continued through Hanover square and Pearl street to about the present Peck Slip, where were the primitive boats of the ferry of those days.

On *Brouwer straat* lived many of the most prosperous citizens. Several breweries there gave its name to the street.

We now come to Bridge street, which was the second street laid out or occupied as such. This street was called "*De Brugh straat*," or Bridge street, from its leading from the Fort to the bridge across the canal, which ran through Broad street.

Winckel street lay parallel to Whitehall, between the present Pearl and Bridge streets. On this Winckel street, or *Shop* street, were five substantial stone store-houses, belonging to the Dutch West India Co. This street has now disappeared, there being no thoroughfare to represent it.

We come next to what is the present Pearl street. Pearl street formed the original bank of the East river—Water, Front and South streets having been all subsequently reclaimed and built. Here was the first settlement; and some thirty or forty little bark or wood houses, clustered along the bank of the river south-east of the Fort, were the nucleus of this great city.

Between Whitehall and Broad streets, Pearl street was called the Strand, " *T'Water*," or at "the waterside." A portion of this street, between State and Whitehall, was also called " *Paerel straat.*"

Between Broad street and Hanover square it was known as at the East river; also " *De Waal*," being so called from a wall or siding of boards to protect the street from the washing of the tide.

On Pearl street, between Broad and Whitehall, in the vicinity of the landing-place, were the residences of the principal traders and merchants.

The old " *Stadt-huys*" or City Hall, formerly the City Tavern, stood on the present northwest corner of Pearl and Coenties Alley. It had a cupola and a bell, which was rung on great occasions, and for the sessions of the Burgo-masters and Schepens, and on publication of new laws.

This old " *Stadt-huys*" was sold at auction in 1699, and the new City Hall erected about 1698, under the English rule, on Wall street at the head of Broad.

The report of a trial held in the old " *Stadt-huys*," before

the Court of Burgomasters and Schepens, has come down
to us. It exhibits the original and primitive manner in
which legal points were raised and justice dispensed, in
that early time.

Jan Haeckins was plaintiff and Jacob Van Couwenhoven
defendant. An abstract of the report reads thus: The
plaintiff demands pay from defendant for certain beer sold
according to contract. The defendant says the beer is bad.
Plaintiff denies that the beer is bad, and asks whether
people would buy it if it were not good? He further insists
that the beer is of good quality, and such as is made for
exportation. Couwenhoven denies this, and requests that
after the rising of the bench the Court may come over and
try the beer, and then decide. The parties having been
heard, *it is ordered* that after the meeting breaks up the
beer shall be tried; and if good, then Couwenhoven shall
make payment according to the obligation; if otherwise,
the plaintiff shall make deduction.

Near the junction of the modern Pearl street and Stone
street, was what was then known as Burger Jorisen's path,
or Burgher's path, in the vicinity of the present Old Slip,
so called after the sturdy blacksmith who lived there.

We next in our peregrinations come to Broad street.

Broad street was called "*de Heere graft*" and "*Breede
graft*," also the Common Ditch.

Above Beaver street Broad street was *de* "*Prince graft*"
and ran into the "*Schaep waytie*," or sheep pasture, before
spoken of.

Our Dutch ancestors, of course, were not happy without
a canal, and accordingly a miniature one was easily

arranged out of the Broad street ditch; a little estuary also ran in there from the Bay. The ditch or canal ran up beyond Beaver street, and also branched to the west, into Beaver street. Its sides were planked in about the year 1657.

Up this canal were rowed and fastened the boats from the farms and market gardens on the opposite shores of Long Island, and the *Boweries*, on the East and North Rivers.

The ditch in Broad street was not filled until after the English occupation in 1676.

We now come to the modern William street.

William street below Wall to Pearl was "*Smee Straat*," afterwards Smith street.

South William street was formerly "*Slyck Steeghie*" or "Dirty Lane," subsequently "Mill Street Lane:" there being a mill erected in the lane, which was originally a *cul de sac*, leading from Broad street to the mill.

We have now again reached Wall street, at the foot of which is the *Water poort* or Water gate, closed at bell-ringing at nine in the evening, and opened at sunrise.

We may for a moment picture to ourselves an assemblage of the good people of New Amsterdam, gathered together at the widow Mietje Wessels' tavern on Pearl street, near Broad, on the celebration of some festival day, say that of their patron, Saint Nicholas, on the 6th of December, or a celebration of the "*Nieuw Jaar*" or New Year.

The assemblage embraces all classes of the citizens. The distinctions of wealth and rank are not drawn so sharply as in larger communities, but a sympathy of interests and of dangers binds together the little settlement, gives stronger ties to fellowship, and produces a comparative social equality.

The oil lamps and the dipped candles are flickering gaily from the snowy whitewashed walls of Madame Wessels' large assembly-room, and the fresh sand is arranged in gay festoons around the well-scraped floor, carefully prepared by the widow's daughters Jannetje and Hendrickje. Old Mingo, the Governor's black slave, who has been lent for the occasion, is tuning his fiddle for the dance; while on benches around the room sit many of the dignitaries and high officials of the settlement.

We take a glance at the gentle sex as it assembles.

We see complexions fair, features regular, and countenance placid—the invidious might call it somewhat inanimate.

The figure is not tall, but healthy and generous. Nature is allowed to have her sway, without unseemly pressure or restriction.

The hair is bound close to the head with a small cap on the back, leaving the dainty ear exposed with its ponderous gold or silver earrings. Large plates of thin gold project from each side of the forehead, and in some cases there is a plate in the middle.

Necklaces, too, hang around many a snowy neck, and at the sides of some hang embroidered purses, with silver ornaments and chain.

Gowns of thick silk, heavily embroidered, with waists of a rotundity that would startle a modern Venus, encase forms that though substantial are agile in the dance, as the glowing and shiny faces, after the active capering then in vogue, amply attest.

Some wear short petticoats, of fine blue or scarlet cloth, or of some gay striped design. Coat-tails, of a darker hue, project in the rear, and colored hose, with lively clocks on the side, encase limbs which attest the solid charms that result from health and exercise.

Some of the more elegant dancers wear petticoats of quilted silk, of varied hue, embroidered with filagree in silver or in gold.

The elderly ladies have about the head the crape or tartanet "*samare*" then in vogue.

The gentlemen appear in homespun, serge, or kersey, or colored cloth; some in velvet or silk breeches, and coat flowered with silver, with, perhaps, gold or silver buttons, and lace neck-cloth, and silken stockings; shoes with buckles of copper or silver, as suits the wearer's taste or means; and some with steel or silver-handled sword hanging by the side.

Among the young *Juffers* or misses, we notice Margrietje Van Cortlandt, subsequently Mrs. Jeremias Van Rensselaer, daughter of the notable burgomaster, Oloff Stevensen Van Cortlandt, who is walking with becoming dignity about the room, with his little boy Johannes.

We notice, also, Captain Martin, Cregrier's pretty daughters, *Lysbeth* and *Tryntje*, with their young brother Frans, who has proudly on his arm Miss Walburg de Silla, with whom the bans had just been published.

Further on is de Heer Direk Van Cleef, the prosperous trader, and his wife Geesje, and their two little people from the Cingel, the little girl in a mob-cap and long ear-rings, and the little boy in knee-breeches and silver-buckled shoes.

And there is the fine lady of the day, Madame Ann Bayard Verlett, wife of Captain Nikolaes Verlett, formerly Ann Stuyvesant, a relative of the Governor, and her three sons, Balthazar, Pieter, and Nikolaes, by her first husband, Samuel Bayard, all of whom became famous men during the English colonial time.

With Madame Bayard is her relative, the beautiful Judith Verlett, who, a few years later, when visiting Hart-ford, was arrested as a witch, and only delivered from the clutches of the ungallant Puritans by the most earnest action of the Governor. Now her witchery is exerted upon her attendant swain, Master Nikolaes Bayard, whom she subsequently married.

Walking with some dignitary of the day, is the proud *Juffrouw* Antonia Van Slaghboom, Arent Van Corlaer's wife, who assumed her former name to show her descent, as being of the house of the Slaghbooms.

Talking with the bride, Mrs. Domine Drysius, we behold Domine Johannes Megapolensis and his wife, Mrs. Magteldt, near whom is her son Samuel, the young Domine, who has just graduated with honor at Harvard University, and her other sons, Direk and Jan. And there, too, is her daughter, Hillegond, carrying her head pretty high, for she is married to no less a person than Cornelius Van Ruyven, the Colonial Secretary.

And here is the elegant Margareta de Riemers, now the

bride of Cornelis Steenwyck, the rich merchant; and young Wilhelm Bogardus, a son of the late Domine, walking proudly with Miss Wyntje Sybrants on his arm, with whom he is soon to enter the bonds of matrimony.

And there is the Don Giovanni of the period, Geleyn Verplanck, who, after many scrapes, finally was permanently captured by the fascinations of Hendrickje, daughter of Madame Wessels, then a young miss of about fifteen.

Here also is *Juffrouw* Van der Donck, widow of Adrian Vander Donck, the Patroon or feudal chief of the colony of Colon Donck, between the Hudson and Zaeg-Kill, or Saw-mill Creek, who, from his Dutch appellation or *sobriquet* of the "Jonker," gave its appellation to the modern Yonkers.

And there is Nikolaes de Meyer, and his wife Lydia—she that was a Van Dyck, daughter of the rich *Schout Fiskaal*, Van Dyck, and at whose wedding it was said a disappointed lover, young De Haas, took the lucky bridegroom by the throat, and would have strangled him had the guests not interfered.

Leaning on the arm of Jacob Steendam, the New Amsterdam poet, we see the gay *divorcée*, Mrs. Nikolaes de Sille, the only recorded phenomenon of that kind in New Amsterdam.

And here, too, is Mrs. Dr. Hans Kierstedt, from the Waterside, and her little girl Blandina, and near them Master Pieter Bayard, who afterwards married the fair Blandina.

And there were the lively young fellows, Stoffel Hoog-

landt and Jan Ter Bosch, and also Conraedt or Coentie Ten
Eyck, the tanner, on the *Heere graft*, who gave his name to
Coenties Slip.

Dancing lustily we see some more of the young girls
and belles of the period—Gysbertje Hermans, and Tryntje
Kip, and Maretje Van Hoorn, and Geertruyd Wyngaerdt,
and Jannetje Hillebrants, and Magdaleentje Van Tellick-
huysen, and Bellettje Plottenburg; all then buoyant and
palpitating with life and joy, now vanished and numbered
with the army of the Past. With them, too, is the stately
Judith Isendoorn, who soon after fell captive to the classic
wooing of Aegidius Luyck, the Latin schoolmaster.

Here is bluff Thomas Hall, the English farmer, from the
"*Smits valley*," near Beekman street, and Evert Duyckingh
and his wife Hendrickje, and Johannes Pietersen Van
Brugh, from the Hoogh Straat, the latter of whom married
a daughter of Mrs. Domine Bogardus.

There, also, walking about in uniform, with a proud
beauty on either arm, is the redoubtable commander, En-
sign Dirck Smit. He who, with a dozen men, had marched
through the then *terra incognita* down to the South or
Delaware river, to capture a Swedish ship; who, with a
little garrison of 50 men, had defended the village of Esopus from the Indians, and had stood a three weeks' siege in
the stockades, and who afterwards fought his way through
the woods and took an Indian fort nine miles inland, just
north of Esopus, and made the great Indian chief *Popo-
gunachen* to flee before him.

And there were the rich bachelors Balthazar de Haert,
Jan Van Cortlandt, and Jacobus Kip, and Johannes

Nevius, the Clerk of the Court ; and also Carl Van Brugh, the Company's " Opper Koopman " or chief commissary.

And Jacob Melyn, son of the former Patroon of Staten Island; and many more of the lads and lasses of the time who we may not further particularize.

And there were solid rounds of beef, and pork, and venison, and *sapaen* and oysters, and *Oly-Koecken* and *Panne-Koecken* in variety.

And there was Antigua rum and brandy punch, and Fiall, Passado, and Madeira wines, and other strong potations that suited the stamina of the time—and kept off the cold of the wintry walk or drive.

The revel, which began at five, was finished by nine— when Captain de Pos with his rattle watch began to go the rounds—and there was a putting on of woollen and cloth wrappers, and "rain cloths," and yellow and red "love hoods," through which peered roguish eyes that often invited some enterprising Jan or Dirck to take a New Year's *smack*, on the home drive to the *Bouwerie*—and soon the guests were gone, the lights out, and the full moon shone down on the glistening snow, piled on high peaked roof, and weathercock, and arms of gigantic windmill that stood like sentinel over the sleeping town, with no noise to break the silence of the night, save its creaking arms as they moaned under the blasts from the bay. Swinging in the moonlight, too, was the sign at the Widow Litschoe's tavern, on the water side, facing the East river, where had been another party of a different character.

There—playing draughts and enveloped in smoky clouds, drinking capacious potations to his Mightiness of Orange

and *de Heer Directeur*, and confusion to the red men and
Spaniards, and swearing big oaths of valor—had been Hendrick the smith from *Brugh-Straat*, and Jacob Schaafbanck
the jailor, Albert Pietersen the trumpeter, and Hendrick
Hendricksen, the drummer, from *Smee* street, and little Jan
Jansen Busch the tailor; which latter, being too noisy in his
demonstrations and pugnacious in his mode of argument,
Hendrick Van Bommel and Jan Jansen Van Langstraat,
two of the night watch, were carrying off, kicking and
roaring, to the jail-room in the *Stadt-huys*, there to finish
the evening's amusements until he could resume his wonted
phlegm.

Outside of the city walls there were various localities of
interest, but time will not allow more than a hasty glance
at a few of them.

Beyond the " *Water-poort* " and city palisades, Pearl
street was continued along the shore, and bore the name, up
to about Peck Slip, of the " *Smit's Valley* " *vley*, or valley.

At about the foot of Peck Slip was the ferry to Long
Island, where the passenger, if he desired to cross, blew
the horn hanging there to summon William Jansen, the
ferry man, who for about three stivers, or half a cent, would
take him over the stream.

Outside of the city palisades, beyond Wall street, Broadway was called the " *Heere-Wegh.*"

Beyond Wall street was the " *Maagde-Padtje,*" or the
Maiden Path, which nomenclature was changed to Green
Lane or Maiden Lane about 1690.

This lane was, under our Dutch ancestors, a rural shady
walk, with a rivulet running through it, and sloping hills

on either side, from one of which looked down Jan Vinge's windmill, on the Damen farm, just north of Wall street.

South of the Maiden Lane stretched the "*Klaarer Waytie*," or pasture field of clover, belonging to the Jan Jansen Damen farm; and near by, a little cascade, formed from living streams, fell through the foliage over the rocks, and delighted the eye of the poet or lover of the period, as he roamed amid these then sequestered shades.

We pass Vandercliff's orchard and *Gouwenberg* Hill, on part of the present Pearl, Cliff and John streets, then a favorite place of resort for the citizen on sultry summer afternoons. There he might rest, fanned by breezes from the bay, and overlooking the romantic wooded shores on the opposite side of the river, and refreshed by a little stream that came singing down its rocky bed along the present line of Gold street.

We pass also *Besteraers Kreupel bosch*, or *Kripple Bush*, since Beekman's Swamp, covering parts of Ferry, Gold, Frankfort and adjacent streets, and arrive at the Park, in those days called the "*Vlacke*," the Flat, or the Commons.

On one side of this passed the main highway leading out of the town to the Bouweries, afterwards known as the Post road to Boston.

To this Common the cows of the inhabitants were driven from the city by Gabriel Carpsey, the herdsman, who, as he passed along Broadway, Pearl street and Maiden lane, blew his horn, and collected the cattle to be pastured, which came out lowing from their various enclosures. On his return along those streets, each respective cow, knowing her home, stood at the gate until admitted, the herdsman again blowing his horn to notify the owner to receive his docile animal.

Passing the corner of Chatham and Duane, we come to the fresh-water pond or lake, called the *Kalck-hoeck*, in subsequent days corrupted into the COLLECK, or COLLECT.

This pond was very deep, one of the most romantic spots on the island, and a favorite resort for the angler and the pleasure-seeker.

Where the "Tombs" now looks grimly down on noisome Centre street, there was presented in those days a charming sylvan scene. Lofty hills, clad with verdure and rich with varied foliage, surrounded the clear waters of the lake, which was fed by rivulets that flowed in through groves fragrant with flowers, and musical with the song of birds. Little pleasure-houses were placed upon the banks and shore, and fairy-like boats skimmed the pellucid waters.

Here the angler pursued his gentle sport, and here the lover of Nature came from the busy haunts below, and found repose and solace amid the peaceful scene.

On this pond, in 1796, then 60 feet deep, John Fitch paddled, to the admiration of the gazing multitudes, his little experimental steamer, about 18 feet long.

North of the lake stretched the range of marsh land, which it was subsequently found necessary to drain through Canal street.

From the Kalck pond a little sparkling fresh water stream, called the "*Ould Kill*," or the "*Varsch Water*," or fresh water, ran over Wolfert's meadow, which covered the present Roosevelt street, and emptied into the East river at foot of James street, which stream was covered by a bridge at the junction of Roosevelt and Chatham streets, in English times called the Kissing Bridge—so called because a certain salute was claimed there by enterprising travellers from their complacent companions.

Near this was the celebrated tea-water pump, whose water was subsequently carried in carts about the city, within the memory of many here.

North of the Kalck Hoeck pond was land called the *Werpoes*, originally granted to Augustine Heermans, in 1651 —about 50 acres—and for a time a plantation for old negroes.

In 1644 the woods were partially cleared between this plantation and the great Bouwery, where was afterwards Governor Stuyvesant's house, between the present 2d and 3d avenues and 10th and 11th streets, about 125 feet west of St. Mark's Church.

There were five other Boweries or farms that had belonged to the Company, between the Chatham Square and Stuyvesant's Bouwerie, that were sold to various individuals.

The above farms were devastated by the Indians in 1655, but subsequently houses were again built on them, and the Bouwery road was established, running at first through dense woods.

We read of one Jansen about this time asking to be released from his tenancy of land near the Bouwery, " as he had two miles to ride through a dense forest."

On the west side of Broadway, between Fulton and a line between Chambers and Warren streets, and extending to the North River, was the West India Company's farm, subsequently confiscated by the English, afterwards known as the Duke's and King's Farm, and by the Crown ceded to Trinity Church.

North of it was the Domine's farm or Bouwery. This is the domain of Mrs. Anneke Jans or Jansen—as has been humorously said, "One of the few immortal names that were not born to die."

This lady was born in Holland and came over early ; her first husband was one Roeloff Jansen, a superintendent at Rensselaerwyck, who subsequently came to New Amsterdam. On the decease of Jansen the fair widow was persuaded to re-enter the bonds of Hymen by Domine Everardus Bogardus. Subsequently, on the Domine's decease, the widow went to Albany, and died there in 1663.

She had eight children, four under the first and four by the second marriage.

Her will is at Albany, dated 29th January, 1663, by which she leaves to her children and grandchildren all her real estate in equal shares, with a prior charge of 1,000 guilders in favor of the children of the first marriage, out of the proceeds of their father's place, viz., a certain farm on Manhattan Island, bounded on the North River.

This farm had originally been conveyed by Governor Van Twiller to Roeloff Jansen. It was confirmed to Mrs. Anneke subsequently by a grant given by Stuyvesant in 1654, and was again confirmed in 1667 by the first English Governor, Nicolls.

The farm consisted of about 62 acres, running on Broadway from Warren to Duane ; it then left Broadway on a northwest course, and ran north along the river. It commonly went by the name of the Domine's Bowery, the upper part above Canal being called the Domine's Hook.

A majority of the heirs, after Mrs. Anneke Jans Bogardus' decease, about the year 1670, made a conveyance of the tract to Governor Lovelace, whose interest in the same was subsequently confiscated for debt by Governor Andros, under orders from the Duke. It was then called the Duke's farm, and was subsequently granted to Trinity Church by Queen Ann.

The claim of the heirs who did not join in the transfer of the property, and their descendants, has been asserted at different times down to the present day, and a right of escheat has also been claimed as against Trinity Church in favor of the State.

The heirs claim that the grant of the tract by *Queen Ann* to the Church was invalid, inasmuch as the Crown had no title to their portion of it.

The first suit we read of was brought by Cornelius Brower, one of the heirs, in 1750, in which he was non-suited, and in 1760 a verdict was rendered against him; and for the rest of the century, in the newspapers of the time, are to be found notices of meetings of the heirs for the assertion of their claims.

In 1807 suit was brought by one Col. Malcolm; one in 1830, by three of the heirs; and other suits in 1834 and in 1847, and also since that date, which all resulted in favor of the church.

We subsequently read of private meetings and mass meetings, at different times, of these irrepressible heirs, who are now daily increasing, in geometrical proportion.

At one of the last grand meetings in 1868, in Philadelphia, delegates were present from five States, and upwards of two thousand heirs were represented, and bonds were issued to pay expenses.

A suit, I believe, is now being prosecuted in the Circuit Court of the United States, for this Circuit, to recover this ancient piece of swamp pasturage, which now is worth many millions, but at one time is stated to have been leased for the annual rent of two hogs.

The church title is not, as is alleged by the heirs, placed upon the deed from a majority of the heirs in 1670 to the English Governor Lovelace, but upon the grant to the church by Queen Ann in 1705, and a continuous and open adverse occupancy and possession by the church, since that time, which possession under a claim of title has made, it is asserted, an indefeasible title.

The heirs in their litigation meet the defence of adverse possession—which, by law, in twenty years ripens into a title—by the plea that Trinity Church does not hold adversely, but merely by a possessorship as tenant in common under the deed to Lovelace by a part of the heirs; and claim the well-known principle of law that one tenant in common holds for the joint benefit of his co-tenants and cannot hold adversely.

North of the Domine's Bouwerie was an extensive swamp, and north of that the tract known to antiquarians as "*Old Jan's* land;" being the land of old Jan Celes, a settler from New England in 1635.

Time will not allow me further to pursue my sketch of the people and places of this our earlier period.

A period which seems to increase in interest as it recedes into the past.

Recent historians have brought forward prominently the courage, the patriotism, and the worth of the Batavian people, co-workers with the Anglo-Saxon in vindicating human rights and extending the area of liberty.

A people, it has been remarked, whose country, created in the midst of marshes, had no solid foundation except in the wisdom of her rulers and the untiring industry of her people.

A people whose learning has given to science discoveries that have proved of lasting benefit to humanity.

A people whose patriotism overwhelmed their land with the floods of ocean to keep it from invasion, and whose courage has never given way under oppression or defeat.

A people who, emerging triumphant from the bloody struggle which for nearly half a century had taxed their life and their resources, established public schools, and gave to Europe freedom of education, of conscience and religion.

A people whose country, in the face of the inhumanity and intolerance of the time, was, like the Jewish altar, an asylum for the persecuted and oppressed; and which, says Michelet, was the bulwark, the universal refuge and salvation, humanly speaking, of the human race.

While New England was burning witches and torturing Quakers, New Netherland was free from delusion, and received within its borders ministrants of every creed.

When Stuyvesant, subsequently, began to persecute the Quaker, his hand was checked. When, also, he made proclamation against outside preaching or conventicles, except in conformity with the Synod of Dort, under a heavy penalty, he was sternly rebuked by his directors.

On one occasion, we read that he sought to coerce the Quakers at Flushing to conform to his ideas of worship, and arrested and transported to Holland one of their principal men, John Bowne. The latter, on appeal to the Home Government, returned in 1663, bearing a letter to the Governor from the Dutch authorities, re-establishing tolerance in matters of religious opinion, in these memorable words: "The consciences of men ought to be free and unshackled, so long as they continue moderate, peaceable, inoffensive, and not hostile to government. Such have been the maxims of prudence and toleration by which the magistrates of this city, Amsterdam, have been governed; and the consequences have been that the oppresed and persecuted from every country have found among us asylum from distress. Follow in the same steps and you will be blessed."

Such were the noble words of this noble land, in opposition to the policy of countries that hid the light of science in dungeons—that governed through the judgments of the Inquisition, and guided minds by the terrors of the sword, the scourge, and the anathema.

I cannot close this allusion to this people, great in all qualities that make a nation, without a reference to the preamble of their notable Declaration of Independence of the Spaniard—issued 1651—the prototype of our own Charter of Freedom. A portion of their Declaration reads as follows: "The States-General of the United Provinces of the Netherlands, to all who shall see or read these presents, greeting: *Whereas*, it is notorious to every one that the prince of a country is established by God as a sovereign chief of his subjects, to defend and preserve them from all injuries, oppressions, and violences: *   *   * And when he does not do this, but instead of defending his subjects, seeks to oppress them, and deprive them of their privileges and ancient customs, and to command them and use them as slaves, he ought not to be deemed a prince but a tyrant; and as such his subjects, according to right and reason, can no longer recognize him as their prince.   *   *   But they can abandon him, and choose another in his place as chief and lord to defend them."

I wonder, Mr. President, in view of this nationality, which is part of our own, which is sympathetic with us in all that constitutes greatness and virtue in nations, which is part and parcel of our history and of our blood,—I wonder, I say, that while the flags of St. Patrick and St. George, on the festal days of those Saints, flaunt their folds over City Hall and public edifices, that, on the festal day of St. Nicholas, no banner is seen to recall our ancient historic time.

Is this ignorance or an incomprehensible partiality?

It is sad to reflect that there is not a thing left to mark the site of this ancient town, with the exception of the little slender scion of the pear tree, that has shivered through the wintry blasts and is now dying, at the corner of the Third avenue and Thirteenth street, whilom the site of a part of the Bouwery of Governor Stuyvesant.

In Europe, each locality preserves with a religious care all remnants of its early history.

But here, Time's effacing fingers, assisted by the inroads of
"Speculation" and Finance, that know no law higher than
gain, have swept away all visible memento of the past.

Nieuw Amsterdam has vanished. The names of some of
the old settlers and denizens, preserved in those of their
descendants, and a few old records in the City and State
Archives, are the only tangible proofs of even the existence
of the old Dominion.

The quaint little city has passed into history.

The once busy and hardy people have left no trace of their
active and earnest life; and even their grave-yard has been
built over and buried from human contemplation.

I have thus, Mr. President, endeavored to fulfill my at-
tempt to present, in a manner, perhaps, too familiar for the
gravity of this body, a review or sketch of our old city in its
primeval days, and to group together some of the personages,
both notable and humble, who preceded us in the occupation
of our island.

I have presented to you little that is new, little that is not
due to the researches of your local antiquarians, at the head
of whom is our respected member, Dr. O'Callaghan.

But it seems as if this association, in the midst of
its more prominently useful researches, would do well, at
times, to review the incidents of the lives and places of
abode of the grave, persevering, just men that preceded us;
to endeavor to keep up a public interest in this the most in-
teresting period of our local history; and to hold up to suc-
ceeding generations the trials, the courage, the industry and
the virtues of our Dutch ancestors.

www.ingramcontent.com/pod-product-compliance
Lightning Source LLC
Chambersburg PA
CBHW031320280626
47169CB00019B/2450